My dear,
let this be your first step
to a lifelong adventure
of learning

Welcome to the farm
where everyone's friends.

They're up with the sun
until the day ends.

They're all excited
to meet you

Let's go and
learn what they do!

Shepherd the sheep
stays warm wherever he goes.

He's covered in **wool**
from his head to his toes.

He can sheer some off
and knit it together,

to make his friends
a cozy **sweater**.

BAA

Coral the Cow

makes **milk** that's sweet and creamy.

Her big brown eyes
are kind and dreamy.

If she looks your way
and lets out a **mo**o**O**

that's her way of saying
'How do you do?'

Henrietta the Hen

is a great mom.

She sits on her **eggs**
all day long.

Even if it's cold
or starts to storm.

she won't move
so they stay **warm!**

CLUCK
CLUCK

Russell the Rooster

wakes up with the sun.

He **CROWS** to say
the day's begun!

There's a lot of work
to do on the farm,
and Russell's job is
to be the **alarm!**

Dolores the Duck
has a lot to teach.

While keeping her **ducklings**
within reach.

She'll teach them to sing
and to **swim.**

She'll teach them
everything!

QUACK

Pippin the Pig
has seeds to sow.

He waters his **flowers**
so they grow!

If he gets muddy,
that's okay.

It's dirty work
gardening all day!

OINK

Turner the Turkey

loves to eat.

He eats all of his veggies
and all of his **seeds**.

If you want to put Turner
in a good mood,

just give him a plate
of good **food**.

GOBBLE
GOBBLE

Gustav the Goose
stirs his **pot**.

Soup or stew,
it matters not.

He's always **cooking**
because it's his dream:

to be the best chef
you've ever seen!

HONK

Calix the Cat
is pretty **smooth**.

You can't even hear him
when he moves.

He puts things he finds
into his **sack,**

then off he goes
with it on his back!

MEOW

Douglas the Dog

keeps watch on the farm.

When he sees something strange
he **BARKS** in alarm!

He's everyone's friend
at the end of the day.

He likes to be **pet**
and he likes to play.

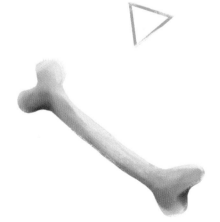

Donald the Donkey
plays in the **hay**.

He's a silly boy
who **laughs** all day.

All he wants is to play
with his friends.

He hopes the fun
never ends!

HEE-
HAW

Orwell the Ox
is big and **strong**.

He can pull a **cart**
all day long.

If the farm wants
to chop down trees,

they ask Orwell
and he does it with ease!

MOO

Gordon the Goat
mows the lawn.

He **eats** all greens
until it's all gone.

Look at the grass,
nice and trim.

This **beautiful** lawn
is thanks to him!

Horace the Horse
never stops training.

He **trains** when it's sun
and he trains when it's raining.

Today he's off
to compete in a **race**.

Everyone hopes
he wins first place!

NEIGH

Harold the Hare
has a date.

He needs to hurry
so he won't be late.

One quick look in a **mirror**
and he's on his way.

Gotta make sure
his **hair** looks okay!

SQUEAK
SQUEAK

Now the sun
is getting low.

It's time to say **bye**
and to go.

We hope you had fun
and made some **friends.**

Be sure to come back
and learn again!

Thank you

for joining us on this adventure. If you
enjoyed this book, would you consider
reviewing it on amazon.com?

(Scan with your phone to review)

Printed in Great Britain
by Amazon